THE SEA
CHALLENGE

The Sea Challenge

BEAR GRYLLS
ILLUSTRATED BY EMMA McCANN

First American Edition 2017
Kane Miller, A Division of EDC Publishing

First published in Great Britain in 2017 by Bear Grylls, an imprint
of Bonnier Zaffre, a Bonnier Publishing Company
Text and illustrations copyright © Bear Grylls Ventures, 2017
Illustrations by Emma McCann

For information contact:
Kane Miller, A Division of EDC Publishing
PO Box 470663
Tulsa, OK 74147-0663
www.kanemiller.com
www.edcpub.com
www.usbornebooksandmore.com

Library of Congress Control Number: 2017946254

Printed and bound in the United States of America
1 2 3 4 5 6 7 8 9 10

ISBN: 978-1-61067-769-1

To the young survivor
reading this book for the first time.
May your eyes always be wide-open
to adventure, and your heart full
of courage and determination to
see your dreams through.

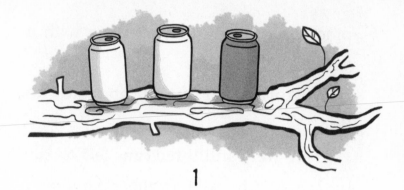

1

TARGET PRACTICE

Chloe held her breath and squinted across the top of her hand at the target.

Thwack.

The rubber band shot through the air and hit the empty can on the branch. It teetered, then toppled to the ground.

"*Yes!*"

"Five out of five?" Her friend Lily was openmouthed. "You're so good at this."

Chloe smiled. It was amazing what

practice you could get at home with a ten-year-old brother.

"My turn," said Mia. "I can totally do this."

There were still three cans left on the branch. Mia hooked a rubber band over her thumb on one hand, and pulled it back. When Mia let go, the band shot forward – and hit her hand.

"Bad luck!" Lily said.

"Yeah, good try, but you had it too far down your thumb," Chloe added. "It couldn't fly over the top like it's meant to. Want to see my special trick?"

Chloe couldn't resist showing off a bit. Just shooting a single band wasn't much good when your brother moved fast. Shooting several all at once, though ...

Chloe got three rubber bands and

hooked them over her thumb, one on top of the other. She slid the forefinger of her other hand through them and pulled them all back together. With one eye closed, she aimed.

"Machine gun!" Chloe announced, and quickly pulled her finger away. The three bands all flew off, *one-two-three*.

It was a good way of hitting a fast-moving ten-year-old.

It wasn't so good at hitting non-moving tin cans. One of them hit a can straight on and knocked it over. The second just made a can totter. The third missed altogether.

The girls watched the second can, holding their breath as it wobbled.

There was a slightly stronger gust of wind and it fell off.

"That was totally the wind!" Lily complained.

"That was totally skill," Chloe said happily.

Mia checked her watch. "Hey, I've got to get to my wildlife welfare course."

"Yeah, come on, Chloe," Lily said. "We should go to the lake – it's sailing next."

"One more …" Chloe said. She couldn't resist a final shot.

The last can bit the dust.

The three girls set off, when Mia paused and looked back.

"Shouldn't we pick the cans up?"

"Leave them," Chloe said. "We'll be late. No one will see them there."

The way to the lake led through a clearing where some of the other campers were celebrating the end of the obstacle relay race.

Chloe had been in the race, but she had tripped and hurt her leg, and hadn't run. She'd only needed a bit of a rest to feel better.

Lily and Chloe got caught up with chatting to some friends about how the race had ended, while Mia headed off for her wildlife welfare activity. A boy with his arms full was heading toward the trash can. He'd been in the race and yelled

at her when she'd gotten hurt, Chloe remembered. He dropped some cans near the trash can and one came spinning toward Chloe. She couldn't resist it. She gave it a kick back.

"Goal!" she shouted as it hit the trash can. Her aim was perfect.

"We should be going," Lily said, laughing. "I'm desperate for the bathroom – I'll see you there, Chloe."

Lily hurried on ahead down the path.

Chloe then heard the sound of footsteps hurrying behind her. It was the shouty tin-can boy. She stood aside to let him get past, but to her surprise he skidded to a halt in front of her. She didn't want to talk to him, but he obviously wanted to talk to her. Or yell at her again. What was his name? Oscar?

Owen? … Omar, that was it.

"Hi?" Chloe said cautiously.

"Uh – hi." Omar held his hand out. "I just wanted to give you this," he said.

"This" was small and plastic and round. She took it and saw that it was a compass.

"Just consider it a gift," Omar added.

"O-kay. Thanks," she said politely. *Strange kid,* she thought. "It'll maybe come in handy in, uh, sailing."

"Well …" He smiled bashfully. He seemed totally different from earlier. "Maybe. Either way, have fun."

And he hurried back the way he had come.

Very strange kid, Chloe thought, but she pushed the compass into her pocket and set off for the lake.

Before long, Chloe could make out the silver shine of the lake through the trees. The water was sparkling in the bright sun.

Then, suddenly, she was distracted by a sound coming out of the bushes at her feet. Curious, she pushed a branch aside with the toe of her shoe.

It was a small baby bird, the size of her finger, at the foot of a tree. Its body was almost featherless. Its head was huge, almost half the size of the rest of it. Its wings were tiny.

Chloe guessed it must have fallen out of its nest in the tree above her.

She looked up and could see a small nest on one of the lower branches, and she could hear more high-pitched cheeping coming from it.

"Aw." Chloe made a face. She would like to do something. She didn't want any animals to suffer. But then nothing she could do would make much difference, she reckoned. Animals die every day.

And anyway, she was in a hurry.

She heard the sailing instructors calling to round people up on the lakeshore, and she didn't want to be late.

"Gotta go," she said quietly to the chick. "Sorry."

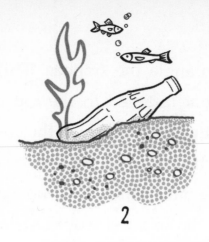

2

INTO THE LAKE

The dinghies were all pulled up on the gravel shore in front of the boathouse. The first job for everyone was to put their mast up.

Chloe and Lily helped each other slot the foot of their mast into a metal track in the bottom of the boat. They pinned it in place and sorted out the ropes that would pull the sail up and hold the boom in place. Last of all, Lily helped

Chloe untangle the trapeze. This was a wire that fastened to the top of the mast, with a ring buckle at the end of it that attached to a canvas harness. When they were out on the lake, whoever was wearing the harness would swing out over the side of the boat, so their weight balanced it against the push of the wind.

It took a lot of practice, but it was the part of sailing that Chloe really enjoyed. It made the dinghy zip along.

An instructor checked their work when they were done.

"Okay," Lily said to Chloe. "Grab the gunwales."

They each gripped the sides of the boat and heaved the dinghy down the gravel into the water. Chloe was wearing shorts and a T-shirt, with the harness around her hips and lower back. The water was soft and cool against her bare legs.

"Um – forgotten anything?" the instructor called.

"Life jackets!" Lily exclaimed. She hurried back to the boathouse to get the life jackets while Chloe waited, standing up to her knees in the water and holding the dinghy in place.

Chloe looked casually around. The lake was three hundred feet across – big enough for a few dinghies to zip around without hitting anyone.

Some boys were on the shore about one hundred fifty feet away, throwing flat stones so that they skipped across the water. A gentle wind whipped the surface up into ripples a few inches high, and the sun was shining warm and bright.

Chloe was excited – she loved sailing and the conditions were perfect.

 *So the wind is from the south?* Chloe thought. She pulled the compass out and glanced at the dial as she felt the wind. Yup. South.

"Where did you get that?" Lily asked in surprise as she came back with the life jackets.

"This boy gave it to me. I thought it might be fun to try it out."

Chloe put on her life jacket and tried to slip the compass into her pocket, but dropped it in the water. The case was made of rubber so it floated. The water was clear and shallow, and Chloe could see the stony bottom of the lake as she bent down to pick it up. Something glinted below the surface. It was a glass bottle and it had been there for some time because it had a very faint covering of weeds. Small black fish were nibbling it. She thought about picking it up.

"So, are we going?" Lily asked impatiently.

Chloe wanted to get some sailing in with just Lily, before they had to get together with everyone else, so she decided just to leave the bottle. It would take too long to go up on shore to the trash cans.

"Okay," she said, "let's catch this wind!"

They gave the dinghy a final shove out into the water and clambered aboard.

Lily took the tiller to steer while Chloe hoisted the sail. It unfolded from the horizontal boom and slid up the groove in the mast. The boom was fixed to the mast by a hinge at one end, so it blew around as the sail caught the wind.

Chloe attached the harness to the wire.

"Okay," she said to Lily. "Let's go."

Lily pulled a rope attached to the free end of the boom and hauled it in against the gentle breeze. Immediately the sail went tight.

The wind chose that exact moment to blow a gust. It caught the sail and in one swift movement, forced the dinghy completely over on its side.

3

CAPSIZE!

Chloe was braced and ready for it.

She felt the harness take her weight as she put one foot up onto the gunwale, then the other. Now she was standing on the edge of the boat, leaning back over the water. The wind couldn't tip the boat over because of her weight, and her weight couldn't pull the boat too far in the other direction because of the wind. The dinghy was balanced.

They zoomed across the lake with Lily at the tiller. Chloe whooped in glee as she trapezed out even farther. This was the best feeling ever. When spray was flying from the bow and the water was zipping past right beneath you, it felt like you were doing a million miles per hour.

They were getting close to the far shore, and running out of lake.

"Get ready to go about," Lily said. She pushed the tiller and the boat began to turn. Chloe quickly swung herself around the mast. As she went, she felt something uncomfortable rubbing against her. Of course, the compass. But there was no chance to do anything about it. She needed to trapeze straight out again, as the dinghy started to pick up speed toward the boathouse.

All the other boats were in the water now. A couple had their sails up and were sailing near the shore. The instructor was waving at Chloe and Lily to rejoin the others.

"Hey, let's have some fun!" Lily said. Without waiting for a reply, she changed course toward a row of floating orange buoys the size of soccer balls. Chloe immediately knew what Lily meant. They were going to slalom, zigzagging back and forth between each buoy. She smiled. "We'll show them how it's done!" Chloe braced herself.

The dinghy shot between the first two buoys and Lily immediately pushed the tiller across. The boat swung around and aimed for the gap between the next two buoys, now leaning the other way. Chloe danced nimbly around the mast to the other gunwale. As she did, she felt the compass press into her again.

She tried to slide her fingers down between the harness and her shorts. Maybe she could adjust the compass a little if she loosened her life jacket? She took off the tape and then ...

"Look out!" Lily shouted suddenly.

One of the other boats was heading right at them. Chloe hadn't seen it because the sail was in the way.

Lily had to push the tiller completely over to get out of the boat's way. The boom swung around with a loud *thwack* and the dinghy leaned over on Chloe's side. She tried to pull herself up, but her hand was stuck in her pocket.

At the last moment she managed to yank her hand out, still clutching the compass.

Then – *SPLASH.*

The dinghy had gone all the way over. She felt herself hit the surface of the lake and water closed over her face.

Chloe spluttered in annoyance as she

surfaced and released the harness from its wire. The life jacket lifted her up so that she floated with her head and shoulders out of the water. She couldn't touch the bottom with her feet. Chloe shook her head to clear the water so that she could see her way back to the boat.

Then, *SPLASH* again. A wall of water hit her from behind and bowled her over. Her body twisted and spun in the middle of a million white bubbles. Her loose life jacket pulled free. And – *yuk!* Her mouth was open and the water tasted disgusting.

Chloe bumped into something solid. The dinghy must have righted itself to be level again. Thank goodness – she could pull herself up before she went flying again. Still blinded by the water in her eyes, she swung herself back onto the boat and clambered to her feet. She watched as her life jacket floated away on the waves.

At the same time, she thought – *waves?* How could there be waves like that on the lake?

And that revolting taste in her mouth – it was *salt*. The water in the lake ought to be fresh.

Chloe shook her head again, then opened her eyes.

The trees that surrounded the lake had gone. One hundred fifty feet away, a long beach of white sand gleamed beneath a tropical sun, and stretched as far as she could see in either direction.

"Lily –" she started to say in surprise. Then she looked down.

She wasn't in the dinghy. She was on a much larger boat. A yacht. White water rushed around her knees.

"We're sinking!" a man's voice shouted.

Chloe whipped her head around. In the cockpit, at the back of the yacht, a man was rapidly pulling at a rope with one hand as he held the steering wheel with the other.

"Time to abandon ship!" he called, as the water swirled around his feet. "Before we go down with this thing!"

FRESH GREEN COCONUTS

Chloe didn't wait to be told twice. She put her hands together and dived over the side into the swirling sea.

The water boiled with bubbles. Her head broke the surface and she started to swim toward the beach. Every few seconds a new wave lifted her up and carried her a bit farther. Soon Chloe was so close to land that she felt her hands brush the sand. She waded the last few feet while the water seethed around her legs.

As soon as Chloe was out of the water, she could feel the sun starting to roast her through her damp T-shirt. It was like a burning spotlight in the blue and cloudless sky. But that didn't worry her half as much as the question of where on earth she was.

The beach rose up to some sandy dunes and a scraggly row of palm trees. Left and right, the white sand stretched as far as she could see. She turned and stared back toward the sea. How had she ended up here?

All Chloe could see of the sinking yacht now was a mast sticking up out of the surf at an angle. The man who'd shouted was wading toward her.

He had a tanned, friendly face and wet, dark hair that was flat against his head.

He held up a dripping backpack.

"I managed to save a few things that might come in handy. Apart from that, it looks like we're on our own."

"Um – right," Chloe said. She looked along the beach again, trying to see her friends. "But *where* are we? And who are you?"

"I'm Bear, and right now we're a long way from anywhere." He smiled. "But I'll do my best to help guide you back home safely." He smiled again. "Don't worry. We'll be okay."

"I'm Chloe." She smiled back. "I really hope you're right because from what I can see we've just lost the boat."

"Well, in that sense, Chloe, you are dead right," Bear added, looking back at the wreck. "But I guess it also means we are in for some *real* adventure."

"You mean, more adventure than jumping off a sinking boat?"

He smiled and ruffled his hair dry.

"That was only the beginning." Bear

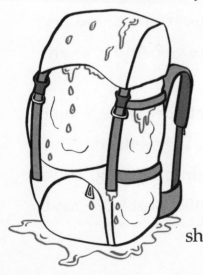 looked up the beach. "Okay. Let's get out of the sun while we assess the situation." Chloe followed Bear up the beach toward the dunes and the shade of the palm trees.

Bear put the wet backpack down and started to pull out waterproof ziplock bags. He opened one up and dug out a hat with a wide, floppy brim, and a cap with a long flap at the back. Bear jammed the cap onto his head and the hat onto hers.

Then he pulled out some clothes in Chloe's size that were like the ones he was wearing – a long-sleeved shirt and pants that looked light but tough.

"Try these," he said, "while I check out the lay of the land."

A moment later he had gone over the dune. Chloe changed into the new clothes and immediately felt cooler as the air flowed between the dry fabric and her skin. She left her old wet clothes in a heap on the sand.

Chloe followed Bear's footprints, and got to the top of the dune just as he was coming back.

"Well," he said, "we're not going that way."

On the other side of the dune was what looked like a field of tall grass. Like the beach, it stretched away in either direction as far as she could see. When Chloe looked closer she saw that it was actually reeds, tall and thin, growing up out of a lake of dark water.

"We can't wade through that," said Bear. "It'll be full of snakes and the leaves will be razor sharp. We're heading along the beach. You used to some distance walking?"

"Not really," Chloe said a little unsurely.

They went back to the shade of the trees and Chloe thought of having to hike in this heat.

"It's a shame salt water tastes so disgusting," she said. "I could really use a drink."

"It doesn't just taste disgusting. It's like poison," Bear said seriously. "It dehydrates your blood and fries your kidneys. I've got a couple of canteens of fresh water in the backpack. But we'll save those for now. There's something else here we can drink."

He smiled and pointed up. Chloe saw green fruit the size of soccer balls hanging in the trees.

Bear took a canvas sheath as long as his forearm from out of the backpack and fastened it to his belt. Then Chloe

watched him shinny up the
trunk. He gripped the trunk
with his arms and shifted his
legs up, then gripped
with his legs and
shifted his arms. It
only took two or three
movements like that
and he was up by the
leaves.

At the top, Bear
drew out what looked
like a very big kitchen
knife from the sheath. He
slashed with it and the fruit
fell down to the sand with
heavy *thud*s.

"What are they?" Chloe
picked one up. It had tough

green leathery leaves surrounding a large green nut.

"Coconuts," Bear said as he climbed down. "Exactly the right balance of salt, minerals and sugar for the castaway."

"Coconuts?" Chloe said in surprise. They didn't look much like the dried-up hairy brown coconuts she'd seen in the supermarket.

Bear picked up one from the sand and cut the leaves away, then lopped the top off with several swift strokes of the big knife. He passed it to Chloe.

"Take a drink!" he said. While he gave a second coconut the same treatment,

she took it in both hands and peered suspiciously into the hole he had made. A cloudy, watery liquid sloshed around inside. Well, she knew what coconut milk tasted like, so she tilted her head back and poured it into her mouth.

Correction. She had *thought* she knew what coconut milk tasted like. This was about a billion times better. She grinned.

"Pretty good, right?" Bear said. "You can't beat it fresh off the tree. Now we'll eat the insides too. It'll set us up for the march. I'll chop the coconut flesh while you clear up." He looked down at her heap of wet clothes on the sand. "We leave things as we find them out here. Respect the wild and it will respect you."

Bear chopped the coconuts with his machete as Chloe reluctantly packed her wet sandy clothes into a bag and put them in Bear's backpack.

"So, how far do we have to go?" Chloe asked as they ate the thick white coconut flesh.

"Well, this beach could go on for a hundred miles or more."

Chloe stopped eating. She stared along the sand. The beach had looked so friendly and cheerful. White sand, blue sea …

Now she saw it in a different light. Hot sun. Salt water. No food. For a hundred miles.

"Oh," she said.

5

WATER, WATER, EVERYWHERE ...

Chloe didn't know how long they had walked already. The sand and sea seemed endless.

The only sounds were the wind and the crashing of the waves. Bear pointed out the high-water mark – a ragged line of dried-up seaweed running all along the beach, left there when the tide went out. He kept them to the smooth, firm

sand between the mark and the breaking waves. It was easier to walk on than the loose, dry sand farther up.

There was other stuff mixed up on the mark too – pieces of wood and general junk that must have been washed up, like plastic bags, bottles and toys. Sometimes Bear would find something useful and put it in his backpack. A length of rope, or a fishing net, or several good pieces of wood. But his backpack started to bulge and soon they just had to leave things where they found them.

Every half hour they drank a little fresh water from Bear's canteens. They really needed it. Even though there was a whole ocean a few feet away, the hot sun meant there wasn't a drop of water in the air. Chloe could feel her face and her hands drying out.

But even though they only took a mouthful of water each time, Chloe noticed the level going down. She wondered how they would fill the canteens up again.

Chloe's hat kept the sun from roasting her brains, and the brim kept her eyes shaded. But it didn't stop light reflecting off the white sand straight into her face, and her eyes were stinging.

Then she saw a flash of red plastic poking out of the sand. She tugged at it and pulled out a pair of children's sunglasses. They were the cheap kind her mom might have bought at a drugstore, but they would do. They were covered in sand, but she washed them in the next wave that came in, then put them on.

"What do you think?" she asked with a proud smile.

"I think you'll make a good survivor," Bear said. "You use what you find, you're resourceful, and use that to keep you going. Smart."

But Bear looked a little sad.

"So ... what's the problem?" Chloe asked.

"Well, I'm just thinking about where those probably came from," Bear responded. "They could have been washed all the way across the Pacific to end up here."

"Cool," said Chloe.

"Only if you think pollution is cool.

Plastic, polystyrene, rubber – they don't dissolve. Nature can't reuse them or recycle them. They just create waste and cause damage to the environment."

Then he smiled. "But we can still use them to help us – and anyway, they look much better on you than inside a fish's stomach."

Just then, something smooth and shiny in the sand caught Chloe's eye. It was the end of a half-buried clear plastic bottle.

"So I guess this won't make you happy either?" she said as she pulled it free. "Now *that*," he said, "will come in handy. We'll take it with us." He put the plastic bottle in his backpack. "Another quick drink, then we need to keep going."

"The fresh water will run out soon," Chloe pointed out as she took the half-empty canteen from him.

"It will. That's why we need to keep alert and our eyes peeled for a water source."

They kept walking. Chloe felt a lot better with the sunglasses on, but she couldn't help worrying about the drinking water.

Soon Bear stopped suddenly, and pointed ahead.

"Look, there's water running down the bank over there. Let's see if it's fresh water."

They raced ahead and sure enough there was a small stream that wound its way from the dunes toward the sea. Bear knelt down and put his finger in the water to taste it. And then he smiled.

"It is fresh. We need to make use of this. We might not find another one of these for a while," Bear said. He pushed his canteen under the surface and it filled with lots of glugs and gurgles.

"Is it safe to drink?" Chloe asked anxiously. She thought of the lake water back at the camp. That looked clear and clean, but they had all been told not to drink it. Animals peed and pooped in the forests, and the rain washed it away, and sooner or later it all ended up in the lake.

"In an ideal world we would boil this

in order to one hundred percent kill any bacteria, but look over there," Bear said. He jerked a thumb at the dunes. "Remember the reeds? Reed beds are a natural filter. By the time the water's come through the reeds to the beach, it's been washed pretty clean. It's amazing how many communities use natural systems like reed beds to clean up their mess – nature is a great inventor, if you look after it."

He checked his watch, then looked around.

"We can take a break here. You rest, and I'll see if I can spot anything from up there."

He dropped his backpack on the sand, and set off to the high dunes at the rear of the beach. Chloe strolled along the stream, down to where the clear clean water soaked into the flat wet sand left behind by the sea. She stood and watched the waves coming in, going out – in, out … it was very peaceful.

Eventually she turned to go – and couldn't. Something was holding her fast.

She looked down. Her feet had disappeared into the sand – she was sinking! Water began to trickle in over the tops of her boots.

Chloe gasped and gave one of her legs a hard tug to get it free. Then the other. But both her legs sank down deeper with a loud sucking noise.

Chloe started to panic. She pulled at her leg again. Then the other. Nothing was budging. If anything, her legs were sinking even farther, as the sand and mud sucked at her limbs.

In a moment she was jerking her whole body from side to side. Instead of pulling her feet free, she fell on her bottom. She put out a hand to steady herself, and then she felt that start to sink as well. She yanked it out immediately.

Chloe's heart began to pound and her mouth went dry at the thought of what might happen. Sinking into the sand, getting it in her mouth, her nose, clogging up her lungs ...

"Bear!" she screamed. "Help! I'm sinking!"

6

CIRCLE OF LIFE

"Stay calm!" Bear came pelting down the dune toward her. "I've got you! Just try to stay as still as you can!"

Chloe trusted Bear, but it took all her self-control to stop struggling. She could feel the cold, wet sand creeping slowly up her legs – she was still sinking.

Bear skidded to a halt a couple of feet away from her.

"You're in quicksand," he said. "The

sand's so wet it can't hold your weight. Lean forward, and lie flat on your front."

"*What?*" Chloe exclaimed. "No! I'll get sucked in!" She thought again about getting sand in her nose and mouth.

"Trust me," Bear said calmly. "Lean forward so that your body is flat on the sand. Your weight will be spread across your whole body instead of pushing down into your feet. It'll help the sand

support you, and then you'll be able to crawl free."

He lay down and reached out a hand. "Look, it's okay. Just crawl across the sand toward me."

Chloe tried not to panic as she lay forward. As soon as she put her hands and arms into the wet sand, she could feel it sucking at them. But she crawled forward until she was flat, and even

though the sand still pulled at her buried legs, bit by bit she felt her feet working loose. She wriggled toward Bear's outstretched hand, until at last his fingers closed around hers.

With one movement, Bear pulled her up and away from the quicksand.

"Good job!" he said with a huge smile. "You kept calm, which is the hardest thing to do. The more you struggle, the more the suction pulls you in."

Chloe took a few deep breaths. Her heart was still pounding and her front was plastered with wet sand.

She tried to brush it off, but it clung to her.

"Just let it dry," Bear said. "An hour or so and it'll fall off."

Chloe just nodded. She couldn't quite make herself speak.

"And I found our lunch," Bear added. "You're going to need some food inside you after that."

They walked carefully around the quicksand and farther down the beach. Chloe's legs were shaking, but she kept going.

Something white and flat, the size of a tea tray, was lying just above where the waves broke. Chloe thought that was what Bear was showing her, until she saw the expression on his face as he picked it up.

It was just more washed-up garbage –
a piece of polystyrene packaging. Apart
from being covered with wet sand, it
looked just like it would have when it
came out of the box.

"Do you know how this got here?" Bear
asked in a quiet voice. "Someone got their
new microwave or TV, but they couldn't
take the time to put this
in their trash can. It's so
light, one gust of
wind
could
blow it
down the
street and
into a stream,
then it could float
into a river, and

then get washed out to sea. So here it is now, thousands of miles from where it started."

Chloe looked at the slab of polystyrene. "But if it just floats, why does it matter?" she asked innocently.

"Because it doesn't *just* float. It breaks up and those pieces block up the stomachs of fish and animals, and strangle them from inside. It absorbs poisons and spreads them wherever it goes Polystyrene never breaks down naturally. And it literally kills the ecosystem."

"The … what?"

"The ecosystem," Bear repeated quietly. "The way all the different animals and plants in an area live together. Plants grow, small animals eat the plants, big animals eat the small animals, big animals die, they decay into the ground and fertilize the plants so they can grow. It's the circle of life – where everything depends on everything else."

Chloe stood there silently, looking at the polystyrene. But with eyes that now understood. It looked so harmless – but it wasn't. She wondered how many hundreds of animals could be poisoned by that one slab.

Chloe thought of the rubber bands she had flicked at those tin cans back at camp – and just left there. She hadn't really thought about what would happen to them. Would they rot, or would they just stay there until some animal ate them and got strangled from the inside?

"But it's impossible to clean up all the garbage in the world," Chloe said as Bear shoved the polystyrene into his backpack. "Even if you pick up one piece there'll be a million more."

Bear started walking again.

"I once saw a turtle with a plastic straw up its nose. About this long all the way up, with just a tiny bit poking out at one end," he said, holding up his fingers about four inches apart. "We do good things not because we can save the world all alone. We do good things because it is right, and because we can. I once saw a seal that had been deformed by the plastic rings from a six-pack of cans," he went on. "When it was a baby it had gotten one of its flippers stuck in a ring – and it kept growing. The plastic cut into its flesh, right down to the bone."

Bear paused.

"To that seal it would have made a difference if someone had picked up just that one piece of trash."

Chloe was quiet. It was a horrible thought.

Bear changed the subject and pointed ahead.

"Anyway, I promised you lunch. Over there."

She looked where he was pointing.

"Ice cream?" she said in surprise.

Dozens of small, green ice cream cones were walking across the sand …

7

UNDERWATER WORLD

Closer up, Chloe could see that the ice cream cones were shells. Very short, spindly legs stuck out of the wide end.

Bear picked up a shell and the legs vanished. Chloe peered into the shell. Something was moving in there.

"These are hermit crabs," said Bear. "They borrow abandoned shells because they don't have their own. We'll keep them for lunch."

Bear took out the fishing net he'd found washed up, and a short piece of rope, and folded the net into a bag. They dropped a dozen or so of the pointed shells into the net bag and used the rope to tie it closed. Then they walked on, with Chloe carrying the crabs.

Eventually Bear stopped walking. There was a cluster of palm trees at the top of the beach and a clump of rocks sticking out of the sea about thirty feet from the shore. The sun was almost overhead.

"We should stop for a couple of hours," Bear said. "We'll have our lunch, and sit out the hottest part of the day."

Bear looked up to check that there weren't any coconuts likely to drop down on them, and then they sat in the shade of the palm trees.

Chloe was happy to rest – walking on sand was so tiring and her legs really ached.

"The next priority," Bear said, "is fire." He picked up a dried-up palm leaf and started to tear it into long strips. "Get all the leaves you can find and do this, will you?"

Chloe was surprised.

"Aren't we hot enough?" she asked.

Bear smiled.

"We're hot, but not hot enough to cook shellfish. We don't know what these guys have been eating, so it's best to cook them thoroughly to kill off any bugs."

While Chloe gathered leaves, Bear sifted through the driftwood he'd collected in his backpack until he found a short, flat piece. He dug a small hole in it near to one edge with a knife. Then he cut a V-shaped notch in the side so that the bottom of the V just touched the hole.

Next he selected a thin, straight piece of wood about as thick as a felt-tip marker.

"How are you doing?" he asked, and Chloe showed him the leaf strips that she had made. He piled them all together, then laid a couple of larger pieces of wood on top of them.

Last of all he put the flat piece of wood on the sand, with the notch right up close to the strips of palm leaf.

Bear then spat in his palms, and smiled when he saw Chloe's disgusted look.

"It will help protect against friction blisters," he said. Bear held the thin stick flat between his hands, and put the tip of the stick into the hole. Then he started to rub his hands back and forth so that the stick began to spin in the hole.

"This is a fire drill," he said as Chloe watched in fascination. "The friction of the drill tip is going to create heat. It will start charring the base plate, and then the embers will drop through the V into these strips of husk."

"Cool!" Chloe replied quietly.

"Then, when we have enough embers, I need you to crouch down and blow very, very gently ..."

He kept spinning as he spoke, working his hands up and down the drill stick. Before long, thin tendrils of smoke

started to drift out of the hole. The tip of the drill had ground up a small layer of the wood into a powder that glowed red.

"Now, blow," Bear said. "Gently."

Chloe crouched down low and blew the embers toward the palm strips. The red glow spread slowly along them and the smell of burning grew stronger.

Somewhere in the pile there was a loud *snap*. Even though Chloe couldn't see any flames yet, the air started to shimmer with heat.

And then it happened. The smoke and heat did their job and suddenly the bundle of dried husk burst into flames.

"We have fire!" Chloe said, sounding so proud of herself. "Are we cooking the crabs now?"

"Almost," Bear said. "But there's one more job first, while I build the fire up …" He pulled out the plastic bottle that Chloe had picked up earlier.

Five minutes later, Chloe was wading out to the rocks that stuck out of the sea. The sand under the water was soft and comfortable between her toes. She had the net bag tied around one arm, and she carried the bottom half of the bottle that Bear had sliced in two with his knife.

The rocks were a little taller than she was and she half swam, half walked. The waves had died down and the sea just rippled around her.

Chloe pushed the half bottle into the

water and looked through it, as Bear had told her to.

"Wow!" she murmured.

It was like wearing a face mask to look at a new world. The bottle pushed through the surface and let Chloe see everything below crystal clear.

Above the water, the rocks were bare and dry. Below the water it was completely different. Small fish moved in and out of seaweed that waved gently in the current. A crab spooked and withdrew into a crevice. Sea anemones were like blobs of red jelly that stuck to the rock, their tentacles flowing. And Chloe noticed a cluster of sea urchins – small black balls, covered with spines like razor-sharp needles. Bear had warned her to stay away from them.

Bear had asked Chloe to look for mussels – gray-blue shells clinging to the rocks. She found a bunch clustered under a ledge, and was about to reach for them, when suddenly she stopped and looked again through her bottle.

"It's like a whole different world," she said out loud.

It was – what was the word Bear had used? – an ecosystem. Everything on these rocks was in balance. If one part died, everything would die. The rocks were all they had, so they all had to survive together.

Chloe saw why Bear cared so much about the trash floating in the sea. The whole planet was like these rocks. If the balance was upset, then there was nowhere else for everything living here to go.

She stared at it in wonder for a little while longer, before she remembered her job. Bear had told Chloe only to get a handful of mussels, not to take them all.

She understood why now. Taking  them all would be bad for the ecosystem. So she reached under the water and pulled a few shells loose, put them in the net and started to wade back to the beach.

Suddenly a spear of red-hot agony shot up through her foot. She stumbled. When she tried to put her foot down again she screamed. It hurt more than anything she had ever known.

Her shouts caught Bear's attention and he came running down to the shore. Chloe blinked back tears of pain as she sat in the shallows and lifted her foot out of the water.

An urchin clung to her like a ball of spiky fire.

Several of its spines were stuck into the sole of her foot and her skin was starting to darken around it.

8

EGGS FOR DINNER

Bear came splashing through the shallows toward Chloe. He saw in a moment what had happened.

"Ow. Sea urchin. That's going to hurt."

He lifted Chloe up and carried her back toward the shade at the top of the beach.

"My foot's going black," Chloe gasped through gritted teeth. She had to grind them together to stop herself from whimpering. It hurt *so much*.

"Don't worry. That's just the sea urchin's natural dye," Bear replied. "The spines hurt because they go so far in, so quickly. They're *extremely* sharp. But not poisonous."

Bear set her down beneath the trees, then gently lifted her foot up and studied it.

"The bad thing about urchins is that the spines have hooks at the end, so I can't just pull them out again without tearing your flesh. But I'm going to do what I can."

Bear picked up a stick and used it to knock the urchin gently. Chloe heard a couple of faint snapping sounds as the spines broke and the urchin fell to the sand.

"That'll stop any more going in, but there's still five or six snapped-off spines stuck in you."

He made sure Chloe was sitting comfortably against the tree trunk and then held her foot carefully.

"The good news is they're just natural calcium carbonate, like your bones. So your body won't try to reject them. They'll just dissolve naturally. The bad news …" He made a face. "It'll take time. Days, probably."

Chloe groaned as she thought of all the miles of beach they still had to walk, and how much the spines hurt when she put her foot down.

"I can't sit here for

days!" she replied. An idea struck her. "Maybe if you made a crutch out of a piece of wood, I could keep the weight off my foot and sort of hobble along ..."

"Yes. Maybe," Bear said. "But let me treat it properly first."

Bear got his canteen and trickled a little fresh, clean water over Chloe's foot. Then he wrapped a bandage from his backpack gently around it.

"Next step is to see if I can find something antiseptic to prevent infection. And for you, the best way to take your mind off the pain is to keep busy ..."

Bear dug a metal pot out of his

backpack and set it on the sand. Then he picked a hermit crab out of the net bag and held it out to her.

"We need to cook these before we eat them. Blow gently into the end."

Puzzled, Chloe pursed her lips and did as Bear said. She blew into the opening in the shell, and a set of spindly, armored legs started to emerge. As soon as she stopped blowing, the legs pulled back into the shell.

Bear laughed, and blew into the shell himself. The crab started to come out again, and this time Bear kept blowing until Chloe could see its body. It had a puny little body and one big claw.

"They only have room for one claw in there," Bear said, "and it's the only part with enough meat worth eating. Boil them in some seawater, and then you can get them out of the shells."

He filled up the metal pot with water and placed it on the fire. Then he handed her the knife, sheath first.

"Here. You're in charge of dinner. Cook the mussels along with the crabs. Any that don't close up when you tap them, throw them away. We don't want food poisoning."

Then he headed over the dunes, while Chloe considered the hermit crabs. She blew again into one of the shells.

It wasn't as easy as
Bear had made it look
to get them to emerge
completely.

As soon as the water
boiled she threw the
crabs in the pot with
the mussels. Then she drained off the
water carefully – and once the shells had
cooled down she used the knife to lever
the cooked meat out of the shell. It took
some time to get the hang of it, but she
had half a coconut shell full of crabmeat
and mussels by the time Bear came back.

"Good work, you!" he exclaimed,
before holding up a slab of brown tree
bark. "I found a cinnamon tree!"

"Cinnamon?" Chloe exclaimed. "Like,
for cooking?"

"Yes," Bear said. "It's a natural anti-inflammatory and antimicrobial. So it'll calm your foot down, and kill off any nasties that got in."

He took a metal cup from his backpack and began to slice thin shreds of the bark into it. Then he poured some fresh water

into the cup, and set it on the fire. Once it had boiled for a bit, he let it cool, then washed Chloe's throbbing foot with it. Then he bandaged it back up. After that he split the urchin open with his knife, and levered out the smelly mess of its guts. Then he scooped out a glistening mass of small pink blobs. "Urchin eggs to go with our meal!"

And the meal wasn't bad, Chloe decided. The eggs were salty, and the cooked crabs and mussels tasted good. They washed it all down with more coconut milk, which was like dessert.

They sat on either side of the fire. Bear had his back to the beach, and Chloe was leaning against the palm tree, facing the sea.

"We'll stay put today," Bear said. "I'll make you a simple crutch to support your foot and you can get used to using it – but meanwhile, take it easy, and give your foot a chance to heal. I'll make up a bed for you out of palm leaves to keep you off the sand tonight. Some of the spines might even work themselves out of your skin by tomorrow ..."

Chloe tried to be brave. The cinnamon

had probably done some good, but the fact was her foot still throbbed with pain. And she hadn't realized just how much the walk had taken out of her. She was going to close her eyes and rest when …

Chloe saw something. She squinted into the sun, then leaned across to see past Bear.

She was right. There *was* something. There was a dark blob on the sea, maybe half a mile away.

"Bear, there's a boat!"

9

SMOKE SIGNAL

Bear shot to his feet.

"Quick! The fire."

"We've got a fire," Chloe replied frantically, and a little confused.

"We need a bigger one. To make smoke to catch the boat's attention. Lots and lots of it."

Bear looked around. Then he got his knife out and shinnied up the nearest tree, the way he had before. But this time the blade flashed at the roots of the leaves. One by one, palm leaves started to fall down on Chloe.

"Put them on the fire carefully," Bear called. "Add two or three at a time."

Chloe fed the leaves into the fire, while Bear continued to cut down more from above. The smoke grew thicker. Chloe quickly had to scoot around to the far side so that it didn't blow in her face.

She kept on adding leaves and the smoke turned into a thick, gray column that rose high up into the air.

"Perfect." Bear clambered back down and helped her put more leaves on. "Dead leaves burn hot and fast, but fresh green leaves still have plenty of water in them, so they don't burn as well."

"They make smoke instead?" Chloe guessed.

"Exactly. Which these are doing nicely." Bear leaned back to look up at the smoke. "You carry on here – I'll see if I can get their attention."

He ran down to the edge of the water and started waving his arms in a big wide, rhythmical pattern toward the boat.

"Hey!" he shouted at the boat. "Hey!"

Chloe kept her eyes fixed on the boat. It wasn't big, less than thirty feet long. There was a small cabin at one end and she could hear the *putt-putt-putt* of a little engine. Had anyone on board seen Bear?

It was impossible to tell at this distance.

Chloe held her breath as she stared out to sea. Even the pain in her foot didn't seem to matter now. Then she remembered she still had her job to do, and quickly went back to putting leaves on the fire.

When she looked up, she blinked. Had she imagined it, or …?

Yes! The boat was turning toward the beach!

They had been seen.

Bear hurried back to her.

"We'll have to swim out," he said, "so they don't run aground."

Chloe pulled herself to her feet as Bear kicked sand over the fire to put it out, and gathered up their few things. He stuck the polystyrene into his backpack.

"What goes around comes around. Let's not leave this here. We do something good for the ecosystem and maybe we get rescued in return," he said with a smile.

Chloe kept her hurt foot off the sand

as much as she could, as Bear helped her walk down to the sea. The first waves broke around her knees. After that, she could swim without putting any pressure on her foot at all.

The fishing boat had come to a halt about sixty feet away. Two men stood on deck, waving and shouting encouragement.

As they got farther from the beach, the waves got ever stronger.

"Keep going, Chloe," Bear shouted. "You are doing so well. Never give up!"

Chloe felt the water lift her up and drop her down again, once, twice. Ahead of her the boat suddenly got lifted up by a bigger-than-usual wave. Then the boat was hidden from view as the wave kept coming at her. Chloe saw the top of it begin to break into foam. She put her head down and held her breath.

The wave broke right on top of her. A roaring mass of bubbles came crashing down onto her head. This time she was prepared for it and kept her body straight as the current battered her body. Then it passed. She lifted her head up. Water streamed down her face and blinded her for a moment.

"Chloe! Almost there. Hold your hand out."

Chloe felt her hand knock something hard.

She stretched out to hang on to the side of the boat with both hands and shook the water out of her eyes.

She was looking straight into Lily's smiling face.

WILDLIFE WELFARE

"Whoops!" Lily said. "I didn't even see that boat until it was too late!"

"What?"

Chloe looked around.

She was back in the lake at camp, holding on to the side of the sailing dinghy. No sign of Bear, or fishing boats, or waves. Her foot felt fine. The instructor was calling them over to the shore.

"Come on," said Lily. "We'd better get going."

Feeling slightly dazed, Chloe pulled herself into the dinghy.

"Don't forget your life jacket," Lily said. "It must have come undone."

Chloe reached down to adjust her life jacket, and felt something digging into her side. The compass was under it.

She pulled it out.

 For a moment it looked like there were five directions on the dial, but that must have been the water in her eyes.

When she blinked it was back to the normal four.

Lily steered them back to the

boathouse while Chloe's mind still spun. It all seemed so impossible now. But she remembered being on the beach for most of a day, though Lily obviously didn't think any time had passed at all.

By the time they reached the shore, Chloe had told herself it must have all been a strange kind of daydream.

The sun came out and sparkled off the water. Chloe winced and shaded her eyes with her hand. "At least you've got those silly sunglasses!" Lily laughed.

Chloe grabbed the plastic sunglasses tucked into the neck of her T-shirt. She put them on ...

Sunglasses?

She snatched them off again and stared at them.

Bright-red plastic, slightly clouded with salt stains.

It was the pair she had found on the beach with Bear! She had never seen them before today.

So, the beach had been real after all.

The rest of the sailing session was a blur to Chloe. At the end of it, she honestly couldn't remember anything they had done. As they put their life jackets away, her thoughts were still full of her trek along a tropical beach.

"I'm going to head up to the store," Lily said, "get something to drink – you coming?"

"Uh – yeah," Chloe said. "I'll catch up."

There was a trash can next to the

boathouse surrounded by dropped wrappers and cans. As Lily hurried off, Chloe thought of Bear, and carefully picked up each piece and popped it into the trash can. Then she set off back up the path.

She smiled to herself. *Bear would be happy, at least*, she thought.

At the same time, she heard a boy shouting behind her.

"Hey! No! Cut it out! *Cut it out!*"

Chloe could hear real fear in his voice. She looked up.

She had seen the boys earlier, skipping stones across the lake. Now a couple of them were laughing and dragging

another boy by his arms down to the water. He was struggling to get free.

"Hey! Boys!" an instructor called across to them. "Knock it off!"

The laughing boys reluctantly let go. The boy immediately leaped back from the water and Chloe could see that he was upset. He stormed off up the path.

The others looked too embarrassed to follow him.

The boy was walking so fast he soon caught up with Chloe. He gave her a sideways sort of bashful look.

"Sorry about that. They're friends, really. I just …" He stopped.

"Hey, it's fine. I get it. We all have things we're nervous about, it's fine," Chloe said.

He smiled back and they started to walk together.

"I dunno. It's just water. I kind of freak out. It's silly, I guess." He smiled at her. "I'm Jack, by the way."

"I'm Chloe." Before she could say any more, they both heard a faint, high-pitched cheeping.

"What's that noise?" Jack said.

They were standing under the tree where Chloe had seen the chick that had fallen from its nest. *It must be down here somewhere.* She knelt and moved the branches aside. There it was. It hadn't gone far.

"Oh, the poor thing!" Jack said, crouching to look at it.

Chloe looked at Jack and the chick, and remembered how she had told herself before that nothing she could do would make much difference in the big scheme of things.

But since then she had met Bear.

She thought of the turtle and the seal Bear had mentioned.

"We've got to help it," she said.

Then she had a brain wave – Mia had been doing wildlife welfare instead of sailing for this afternoon's activity!

"Jack, do you know any of the wildlife welfare leaders?" she asked. "Could you go and find one? I'll stay here and guard it, and make sure a cat or something doesn't get it."

"Sure."

Jack quickly ran off back to camp.

While Chloe watched over the chick and waited, she thought about Jack. She felt a bit sorry for him – having friends push him like that, yet also missing out on all the fun he could have if he could swim.

Chloe wondered what Bear would say to Jack, if he was here.

Jack came back after a couple of minutes with the woman who ran the camp's wildlife welfare course. She was carrying a folding ladder and other pieces of gear.

Chloe showed her the chick on the ground.

"Now, let's see this nest."

The woman unfolded the ladder and attached it to the branch where the nest was. Then she carefully climbed the ladder, while Chloe gently picked the chick up. Chloe passed it up to the lady, who tipped it back into the nest. Then she smiled down at Chloe.

"Well done! There's three of them up here. The mother might come back, so we'll leave them where it's safe and not interfere too much. Sometimes humans can make things worse not better. But we'll keep an eye on them in case she doesn't return."

The woman climbed back down again and

folded up the ladder. She gave Chloe a smile.

"You're not in my wildlife welfare group, are you? Well, I think you've earned a badge anyway. I'll see that you get one."

Chloe blinked. She really hadn't expected to get a badge. She had just been doing what was right. Making a difference in the small things.

The woman headed off back to camp. Chloe and Jack walked after her.

"Well done," Jack said with a smile.

"Thanks. I wasn't expecting a badge! What's really weird is, this morning I wouldn't have cared."

Jack looked interested at her honesty.

"So what changed?"

Chloe laughed nervously.

"I met ..." She stopped, and bit her tongue. She had been going to tell Jack about Bear, but how could she? He'd think she was crazy.

But then suddenly Chloe was absolutely certain Bear could help Jack with his fear of water. After all, he had helped her, and she hadn't even realized she had a problem until then.

She still had the compass in her pocket. She took it out and looked thoughtfully at it. She remembered she thought she had seen five directions on it, but now it just had four. But she was sure it had something to do with meeting Bear.

"Oh, cool," Jack said. "A compass. Can I see?"

"Sure."

She passed the compass over to Jack.

"Actually, you can keep it," she said. "Just consider it a gift."

The End

Bear Grylls got the taste for adventure at a young age from his father, a former Royal Marine. After school, Bear joined the Reserve SAS, then went on to become one of the youngest people to ever climb Mount Everest, just two years after breaking his back in three places during a parachute jump.

Among other adventures he has led expeditions to the Arctic and the Antarctic, crossed oceans and set world records in skydiving and paragliding.

Bear is also a bestselling author and the host of television programs such as *Survival School* and *The Island*.

He has shared his survival skills with people all over the world, and has taken many famous movie stars and sports stars on adventures – and even President Barack Obama!

Bear Grylls is Chief Scout to the UK Scouting Association, encouraging young people to have great adventures, follow their dreams and to look after their friends. Bear is also honorary Colonel to the Royal Marine Commandos.

When Bear's not traveling the world, he lives with his wife and three sons on a barge in London, or on an island off the coast of Wales.

Find out more at **www.beargrylls.com**

Test your survival knowledge!

1 Why shouldn't you drink seawater?
a) it tastes disgusting
b) it will dehydrate you
c) fish pee in it

2 Where is the best place to walk on the beach?
a) along the seashore, wading in the surf
b) in the dry sand, so you don't get wet
c) between the high water mark and the shoreline, on firm sand

3 You're stuck in quicksand and sinking! What do you do?
a) lie forward and put your whole body down
b) use your hands to dig your feet out
c) wriggle and pull as hard as you can

4 How can you attract the attention of a boat going past?
a) swim out toward it
b) climb a palm tree
c) make thick smoke from a fire

DID YOU KNOW?

Hermit crabs have to get new shells as they grow bigger. Sometimes they exchange them with other crabs ... and sometimes they fight over shells!

Coconuts are not just good for eating and drinking. Coconut leaves can build a fire, be made into brooms or thatch for roofs, or woven into mats. Everything you need for island survival!

Sea urchins are also called "sea hedgehogs" because of their spiky appearance. Their spines protect their delicate insides, which are delicious to other marine predators ... and humans. In many countries sea urchins are an expensive delicacy.

Experience all the adventures ...

AVAILABLE NOW